MONKEY FACE

story and pictures by
FRANK ASCH

Parents' Magazine Press · New York

To Dr. Billé Pritchard

Copyright © 1977 by Frank Asch
All rights reserved
Printed in the United States of America

Library of Congress Cataloging in Publication Data
Asch, Frank.
   Monkey faces.

   SUMMARY: When Monkey shows his drawing to
his friends, each one suggests a slight improvement.
   [1. Drawing—Fiction. 2. Animals—Fiction]
I. Title.
PZ7.A778Mo   [E]   76-18101
ISBN 0-8193-0862-5   ISBN 0-8193-0863-3 lib. bdg.

One day at school, Monkey painted a picture of his mother.

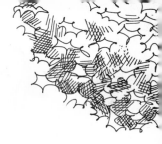

On the way home, he stopped to show it
to his friend, Owl.

"Nice picture," said Owl, "but you made
her eyes too small."

"How's that?" asked Monkey.
"Much better," said Owl.

When Monkey saw Rabbit sunning himself,
he held up the picture for him to see.

"Looks just like her," said Rabbit,
"except the ears are a bit short."

"How's that?" asked Monkey.

"Big improvement," said Rabbit.

At the river bank, Monkey found Alligator and showed the picture to her.

"Pretty," said Alligator, "but she hasn't got much of a mouth."

"How's that?" asked Monkey.

"Beautiful!" said Alligator.

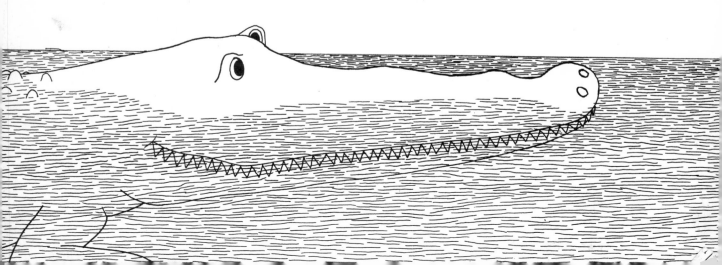

As he walked on, Monkey met Elephant
and showed him the picture.
"Good likeness," said Elephant. "But
her nose is almost invisible."

"How's that?" asked Monkey.

"Unforgettable," said Elephant.

Monkey couldn't wait for Lion to see his picture.
"You're a born artist," said Lion, "except for
one thing—you've forgotten her fluffy mane."

"How's that?" asked Monkey.

"Most becoming," said Lion.

When he was almost home, Monkey saw Giraffe
and let him look at the picture.
"Nearly perfect," said Giraffe, "but her neck
needs to be a little longer."

"How's that?" asked Monkey.

"Truly elevating," said Giraffe.

Monkey ran the rest of the way.
His lunch was all ready and his mother
was waiting for him.
"Look what I made in school today," said Monkey.
"A picture of you."

"I love it!" said his mother.

"Just the way it is?" asked Monkey.

"Just the way it is," said his mother. And she
hung it on the refrigerator for everyone to see.